The Power in the Pain

The Power in the Pain

Marian Kennedy-Brooks

American Literary Press, Inc.
Five Star Special Edition
Baltimore, Maryland

THE POWER IN THE PAIN

All scripture quotations are taken from the
King James Version (KJV) of the Bible.

Library of Congress
Cataloging in Publication Data
ISBN 1-56167-620-9

Library of Congress Card Catalog Number:
00-104289

Published by

American Literary Press, Inc.
Five Star Special Edition
8019 Belair Road, Suite 10
Baltimore, Maryland 21236

Manufactured in the United States of America

DEDICATION

This book is dedicated to the memory of my late daughter, CoCo. Her sudden death pushed me into an abyss of unimaginable pain. It was there that I saw Jesus. Pain moved me closer to Him, and Pain caused me to stay close enough, long enough, so He could gently whisper to me the words found on these pages.

...And when I lift mine eyes towards Heaven,
A tear-soaked gaze to the sky
It is there that I catch a glimpse of you,
"I'm all right, Mommy, don't cry."

Courtney Noelle Thompson
1988-1993

ACKNOWLEDGEMENTS

With grateful appreciation, I would like to acknowledge everyone whose love and undying support made this work possible…

First, I would like to thank my Heavenly Father. I am extremely humbled that You would speak such life-changing words in my spirit, and trust me with such an important endeavor. I am nothing without You.

Thanks to the family of American Literary Press, Inc. Every one of you has been an invaluable source of help and support. Thanks for taking a chance on a substitute teacher. I pray God's richest blessings on the entire corporation for the kindness shown to me.

MICHAEL…You have believed in me with such unwavering conviction that you have caused me to believe in myself. Thanks for immediately putting me to work when I shared this vision with you.

RODNEY…You are my first-born. You have been with me the longest; thanks for being your own person, with an uncompromising belief system, and the courage of your own convictions.

ASHLEY…You remain my surviving daughter, my genuine replica. You make me laugh. It has been my duty to be your mother, but it has been my honor to be your friend.

JOHN 2…You will always be my baby boy. You have grown to be so strong and determined. I deeply respect the gentle and sensitive spirit that you have allowed the Lord to give you.

To my brother and sisters, thanks for allowing me to develop and grow into the 'strange bird' that is my lasting legacy from our mother.

Thanks, Dad, for keeping my wrinkled poems in the pocket of your jacket. I am sure this book will cause a bulk there, too.

CHAREESE...You have been my closest friend, confidante, and prayer partner for over 20 years. Together, we have believed God for miracles; the very best is yet to come!

MOTHER TALLEY...Thanks for being my spiritual mother, and teaching me to become a Woman of Purpose. You were the first one to tell me that I was given, but I was also sent. Mom, I finally got the lessons you have so tirelessly instilled in me.

Finally, I would like to extend my heartfelt thanks to three people who have inspired me beyond words, three Men of God whom I have never met, but I feel I have always known...

BISHOP T.D. JAKES, your videotape, "Creative Concepts", completely revolutionized my entire existence. It was while listening to that sermon I sensed the creative move of God so strongly, that it caused me to plead, "Give me a child, lest I die."

BISHOP DONALD WRIGHT, this book was birthed while I was a member at your church in Washington, DC. This book resulted when I obeyed the charge of my Pastor.

PASTOR ED MONTGOMERY, your series, "Heaven In Your Heart", was my weekly motivator during the penning of this text. The fresh and insightful concepts you shared caused an irrevocable shake-up in my spirit. I shall never be the same.

CONTENTS

BEFORE YOU BEGIN

The information contained in this book is not intended merely for information sake. While I assert that there is a level of power available before the pain has passed, I want all of my readers to understand that this book is not a quick-fix remedy for pain or a ticket to avoid pain. The principles contained in this book are designed to aid the reader in a personal quest towards God.

If you are a person who is not committed to spending quality time before the Lord on a consistent basis, this book will not offer you any real insight. The truths in the volume can only be appreciated to the extent that the reader resolves to wait in the presence of God for the wisdom to grasp a real understanding about the power in the pain.

There may be some unfamiliar concepts contained in this book; you will find it helpful to read the scriptural references thoroughly while studying each lesson. I have tried to explain all words and phrases that I thought would impede your complete understanding of each section. Please keep your personal dictionary handy in order to amplify any points.

Finally, I want to encourage all of my readers to study this book when you have set aside time to ponder, reference, and pray about every single lesson. This book was written at the feet of Jesus, and only at His feet can this devotional be clearly illuminated. I commit to agree with you, the reader, in prayer so that the precepts included in this text can become attainable for you.

It is my heart's desire that you go through your experiences, equipped and strengthened, that you will be able to personally access **THE POWER IN THE PAIN!**

INTRODUCTION

So much has been written about the power that is available to believers when they have endured the inescapable pain that living this life brings. We sing songs about it, we hear sermons about it; we believe that after the suffering is over, we will wear a crown. We bestow certain nobility upon those individuals who have persisted through unimaginable hardships, looking only to the promise of heaven as an eternal reward.

I thoroughly agree with the concept that an everlasting wealth of power awaits the believer after the pain is over, but I have come to realize that there is a place of power available to the faithful children of God within the throes of pain.

This book was birthed one Sunday in a church service. My pastor, Bishop Wright, exclaimed, "I know it hurts, but squeeze the power out of the pain!" My spirit quickened within me, and I immediately became interested in how to access my personal pain power-stores.

There is a degree of power that is only attainable to the willing heart that dares to squeeze the power pump before deliverance has been realized. This is the point in our development when we cooperate with the Father and invite the assistance of His spirit to reach our destinies.

This book is intended to be a devotional tool that women (or men) can use as an aid in their personal study of the Bible's prospective on pain. The text is divided into four sections, and each section can be completed within a five-day week. The entire study can be completed in one month.

Please take the time to reference all of the scriptures and record your daily impressions. This will help you become more familiar with the topics, and serve as a source of encouragement later as you review your answers and chart your growth.

We can become women of God, with the power to inspire our mates, equip our children, and affect change in our communities.

We will no longer complain of our circumstances, or succumb under the weight; we are wailing women, blazing paths to greater works through Christ Jesus. Gone are the shrinking Violets, reduced by the stress of life; we are rising to the clarion call which beckons our immediate response.

Let us rally the troops!

THE PAIN

Pain is any mental or physical discomfort or distress. Pain is usually an unwelcome intruder in an otherwise peaceful existence. We endure that which we can no longer avoid.

Pain is broad in its context and vast in its reach. It is the common denominator that unites us all; we all have pain, we all want to be free from pain, and we all try to minimize the effects of pain.

Personally, I have tried to tolerate the inevitable painful season until it has passed. Recently, I have been learning to appreciate the significant power available to me *in* the pain. The greater the pain, the greater the power.

I am now learning to respect the role of pain in my life, and to admit that God is in supreme control of my entire existence.

There are three principle forerunners to the power in the pain. They are prerequisites, and all must be completed in order to access power. We will explore each component in order to move closer to our power store.

Process is the events or phenomena in our lives. These produce a change in us, which eventually leads to a particular result. As we will discover, all three elements-phenomenon, change, and result must be realized in order to have a completed process. All roads of process lead us back to God, for God is our source. We are guaranteed a more intimate acquaintance with our Father when we commit to the completion of our process.

Purpose is an objective that is gained in the pain we must suffer. God is using our experiences to foster character and fortitude in all of us.

Promise is our God-given reason to expect a specific improvement or success. All of our promises are found nestled in the Word of God. Where a purpose is identified, a promise is assuredly implicated.

Power is the effective ability to take an action. Power surpasses a mere desire to act, when we complete this lesson, we will be effective in our actions!

I continue to learn metamorphic lessons every day and I invite you to journey with me as we complete our process, identify our purpose, implicate our promise, and activate **THE POWER IN THE PAIN...**

PROCESS IN PAIN

"BUT THE GOD OF ALL GRACE, WHO HATH CALLED US UNTO HIS ETERNAL GLORY BY CHRIST JESUS, AFTER THAT YE HAVE SUFFERED A WHILE, MAKE YOU PERFECT, STABLISH, STRENGTHEN, SETTLE YOU."
1 PETER 5:10

Day One

TRIBULATION
"These things I have spoken unto you, that in me ye might have peace. In this world ye shall have tribulation: But be of good cheer; I have overcome the world." John 16:33

Tribulation is the pain we feel because of some oppression or persecution. It is our internal reaction to an external affliction.

What we need to understand about tribulation is its source. Our verse clearly tells us we get tribulation *in this world*. We must never believe that tribulation is God's divine penalty for sin; we suffer tribulation because we are present in this world.

I wondered how we could have any sense of peace when we are told that we will have to suffer the horrendous pain of tribulation. But then I found the answer as I stared at this verse; we are not only in this world, but we are also in Jesus. When Jesus overcame the world, then everything *in Jesus* overcame the world. Are you sure you are in Jesus? If you can answer a resounding "yes", than you are eligible for the inner freedom from anxiety found in the words of Jesus.

One glaring example of the phenomenon of tribulation is the story of the children of Israel(Exodus 1). The basic elements of tribulation can be found within this text. There, we find the general climate of this phenomenon. Oppression or persecution will always occur within a power structure; an authority initiates the offense. In verse 1, we learn that the children of Israel came to Egypt from some place else. They had been extended a temporary courtesy because they were kin to Joseph, an Israelite who became an Egyptian ruler. When Joseph died, the original system was reinstated, and the reprieve was lifted. The children of Israel were now subordinate instead of coordinate in relation to the Egyptians.

Nestled within this cultural demarcation is the first of three precursors to oppression: difference. The recurring theme throughout Exodus 1 is the marked difference between the children of Israel and the Egyptians. It didn't seem to matter how long this nation had resided in Egypt; they were still considered visitors, even intruders in this land.

Next, we see that the Egyptians noticed the growth of the Israelites (verse 9). Finally, we note the potential of the children of Israel (verse 10). Since we outlined the climate and seeds of oppression, what causes its fruition: fear! Fear will cause an authority to enslave your difference, growth and potential.

We must read the entire first chapter set before us in order to uncover the place of peace within the devastation of tribulation. *"And God looked upon the children of Israel..."* there is no tribulation that will escape the sight of God; God sees us! But, when God peered over the balcony of Heaven, just what did He see? Verse 12 offers the pivotal quality of the children of Israel: *"But the more they afflicted them, the more they multiplied and grew."*

Let's explore the change that tribulation produces.

PATIENCE

"And not only so, but we glory in tribulations also: knowing that tribulation worketh patience." Romans 5:3

Contrast Exodus 1:12 with 1:16. The children of Israel experienced a veritable racial explosion, as opposed to the racial extinction the Egyptians had intended. This must have caused them considerable distress, especially since the growth of the Israelites was directly related to the oppression of the Egyptians; the more they were afflicted, the more they multiplied!

Patience is capacity to persevere without complaining. Patience is not an answer to prayer; it is a result of tribulation. The pain of tribulation is sure to sharpen the human capacity to continue on a course; if it doesn't kill you, you are stronger for having endured.

Exodus 2 gives us a glimpse into the survival instinct of the children of Israel: they wanted to live! It would seem that since the Israelites were faced with the dehumanizing conditions of slavery, the last thing they would do is reproduce. But, what the oppression of the Egyptians produced in the Israelites was an unextinguishable will to continue to live. We can conclude that, since the climate of slavery does not invite democracy, there was not a suggestion box placed in the field, soliciting the opinions of the Israelites on their living conditions. But, with what we now know about patience, we can see that the internal reaction of the Israelites to the external affliction of the Egyptians was their determination to continue to grow. Israel did not merely grow by addition; they swelled by multiplication!

When God saw the Israelites, He saw an amazing race of people, refusing to become extinct. He was able to see that these people had developed the capacity to live in cruel and unusual conditions, and persevere.

Do you go through oppression or persecution with a steadied determination to continue without complaining, or does the unfairness of your lot cause you to give up and die?

While tribulation is certainly a normal response to the pain of oppression or persecution, going through tribulation is a sure way to get through tribulation.

Therein lies the gem of patience, a precious stone of unwavering endurance. It will cause God to look down and see us; we are people of persistence and fortitude, sure candidates for the powerful result of this process.

THE PROMISE OF GOD

"For ye have need of patience, that, after ye have done the will of God, ye might receive the promise of God." Hebrews 10:36

The promise of God was for the children of Israel to inhabit the land of Canaan, as He had spoken to Father Abraham (Genesis 12:7). But, the road to promise was paved with difficulty. The Israelites needed something to ensure their entrance into the land of promise; they needed some special skill. What could empower this nomadic nation to make the journey from Egypt to Canaan? We need only to glance at our key verse to see the tribulation result: the promise of God! The human connection between the will of God and the promise of God is patience. In order to receive any promise of God, there must be a commitment to the journey, and commitment requires concentration. Do you see the value of patience? Patience is our capacity to continue without complaining, because complaining inhibits concentration. The energy expended whining about the circumstance saps the inner focus that is critical for the trip.

What was the will of God concerning the children of Israel? Well, God issued several mandates on the way to Canaan, but the basic will of God is spelled out in Psalms 107:8: He just wanted the praise of His people, a simple "thank you". The only surefire way to maintain a patient attitude is to become a praiser, because praisers do not complain.

For purposes of this lesson, we will look a particular set of instructions God gave to the Israelites, with the promise that resulted. In Numbers 13:1, the Lord commanded Moses to send a contingent of spies into Canaan, the land of promise. After 40 days, the conclusion was drawn, this was indeed a good land (verses 23,27). Now, you would think the children of Israel would begin to praise the Lord for the abundant land that was to be their habitation, because that is what a praiser would do.

Look at Numbers 14:2 "*...would God that we had died in this wilderness...*"- **WHAT**? Is this the same race of people who managed to pull off the human paradox described in Exodus 1? Okay, let's review: the Egyptians' systematic assault on the Israelites could not induce their death. In fact, they developed the patience that enabled them to even multiply, to the chagrin of their oppressors. The Lord delivered them out of the hand of their enemy, and led them on a trek towards the land of promise, which, by all accounts, was exceeding good; *now* they want to die, because the trip is difficult? Again, I ask, what? If there was any time this race of slaves should have died, it would have been at the hand of the cruel Egyptians. Our lesson has shown that the internal reaction to the external affliction of tribulation produced a capacity to persevere without complaining. They were well on their way to Canaan, now they have decided, "Gee, this is too hard, I think I'd rather die." This shift comes from the loss of patience; the children of Israel have begun to complain, and complaining has weakened their resolve for the journey.

Our key verse clearly states that patience is essential to the receipt of the promise of God. The lack of patience on the part of the Israelites has effectively cancelled out all of the years of tribulation.

We must retain our patience. Patience is a skill, a precious quality that cost years or even generations of extreme tribulation. This battle-scar is our eternal proof of the pain we have suffered. Cherish patience, and never let it go.

Lest we doubt the validity of our key verse, let us revisit the children of Israel. Although the majority of the spies brought back a faithless report, there was one man who believed in the hope of the promise (Numbers 14:8). His name was Caleb, and he was already 40 years old when he went hiking (Numbers 13:30). He refused to relinquish his patient attitude. There was another 45 years before Caleb actually received his portion of the promise of God (Joshua 14:13).

Whew, 85 years old, and then a promise-receiver; no wonder he had need of patience.

There is a promise in the heart of God for every one of us, but we have need of patience in order to receive it. As unpleasant as tribulation is, it provides the incubation for this valuable commodity.

REFLECTIONS...

Outline your own personal tribulation, with your point of patience, and your received promise. If you have not completed your process, and received your promise, what can you do differently?

Day Two

AGONY

"And being in an agony he prayed more earnestly: and his sweat was as it were great drops of blood falling down to the ground." Luke 22:44

The story of Jesus' Gethsemane experience offers us some valuable insight into the phenomenon of agony.

In Matthew 26, we find the elements of agony, and how important it is in our development.

First, agony will move you to a place of prayer (verse 36). Secondly, agony will cause you to feel a need for companionship (verse 37). Finally, agony is extremely painful and causes distress (verse 38).

The fundamental discomfort beneath the weight of agony is that agony is an internal battle we wage with ourselves when we are faced with dichotomous feelings: we need to do something that we do not want to do (verse 39). We may read this passage and attribute Jesus' resolution to his divinity, but the place of inner conflict is clearly human. Jesus, the man, needed to do the will of His Father; but He did not want to suffer the brutal death that awaited Him.

Let's look deeper into this experience. Jesus, recognizing that prayer was crucial for this process, went to Gethsemane. Because He had brought friends along for support, Jesus became disappointed at their apparent lack of interest (verses 40, 43). Jesus has unlocked the truth of agony: the work of agony is profoundly personal. Even close friends and trusted companions cannot fully grasp the urgency of your agony process. Do not become disheartened when your cronies become heavy-eyed when you are so obviously distressed; Gethsemane is so private that there isn't enough room for both you and even your most ardent supporter. Notice Jesus took friends *to* Gethsemane, but He, alone, went *in* Gethsemane (verse 36). But, why is agony so extreme?

Jesus prayed so intently that His sweat was as great drops of blood: agony is hard work! Jesus was completely spent in prayer; the work of Gethsemane is a rigorous exercise that will require all of your attention. There is no eye-blinking resolution in the process of agony; we need all of the power that Gethsemane has to offer.

Jesus prayed, seemingly reached a conclusion, went to His disciples, and returned to agony. He repeated this sequence two more times (verses 39-44). As tedious as agony is, there really is no substitute for its completion.

Eventually, you will experience change in this process. Let's continue our investigation of what the extreme pain and distress of Gethsemane will accomplish.

SURRENDER

"Then they took Him, and led Him, and brought Him into the high priest's house. And Peter followed afar off." Luke 22:54

Surrender is the choice to submit yourself to the power of another. It is not an act done when your back is against the wall, and you have exhausted all of your other resources. It certainly is not a last-ditch effort, effectually pronouncing your powerlessness. Surrender takes place in the will of a man; without this choice, we would be victims of subjugation.

We can turn back to Matthew 26:39-44, the place of the internal conflict of Jesus. At first glance, we may think the change of surrender has occurred in verse 39, when Jesus uttered, *"Nevertheless..."* But Jesus got up, went to His disciples, and went back to pray the same prayer: Jesus was still agonizing. Surrender is the point when the entire inner dichotomy has been resolved, and the focus has become singular. It is the place in our walk with God when we can accept the sleep of our friends, but continue to move towards the course that has been set for us. Look at Jesus' initial reaction to the slumber of Peter in verse 40; He was disturbed by the lack of interest. Jesus fully understood the significance of His agony in Gethsemane, but others could not. The disciples spent intimate time alone with Jesus, even enjoying a final meal in His presence, but when it came to the urgency of this hour, they were simply too sleepy; it was as if they could not understand what all the hoopla was about.

Look at verse 45 to see the reality of surrender, *"... sleep on now..."* Jesus had finally surrendered when He was poised to do what He needed to do, refusing to be distracted by the torpor of those around Him. Next, we see the attitude of surrender, *"... the hour is at hand..."* Jesus was willing to face what His agony had prepared for: a man's got to do what a man's got to do.

THE WILL OF GOD

"When Jesus therefore had received the vinegar, He said, "It is finished": and He bowed His head, and gave up the ghost." John 19:30

Here is where the process of agony will lead us all: The will of God. Hebrew 10:7 offers the reason for the agony of Jesus in Gethsemane, He came to the earth to do the will of His Father. You may ask yourself, "Gee, Jesus healed the sick, and raised the dead. He performed many miracles, wasn't that the will of God"? Here, it is important to distinguish the work of God from the will of God. Jesus was given to the world to perform the work of God, but He was sent to the world to do the will of God. We can ill-afford to substitute the work of God for the will of God. God's work is our *function*, but His will is our *focus*. We were all given, but we were also sent.

Now, let's turn to Matthew 27. The crucifixion of Jesus was particularly gruesome. If you haven't already read the entire account, please take the time to do so (verses 27-50). There is only one way to describe the toll this horrifying death had on the human body of Jesus: agony! What made Jesus endure such suffering in His body when He could have summoned an angel-squad to rescue him (Matthew 26:53)? Gethsemane! If Jesus had not stayed in Gethsemane, praying and agonizing, He could not have maintained the mental solidarity needed to continue to die until He could proclaim, *"It is finished"*. Mere function is not enough impetus to cause any person to suffer such a macabre death; you must be clearly focused.

We must never attempt the result of the will of God without the phenomenon of agony. Gethsemane is the backdrop of the most powerful time in the human life of Jesus. There, He summoned His courage; there, He sharpened His focus.

As redundant as the prayers were that Jesus prayed, Jesus needed the time to work through all of His internal conflicts. There are no cliffnotes; the road to the will of God will have definite pathways through Gethsemane.

Look at Matthew 27:46. Jesus did not die on the cross in His divinity: this was a man who cried out to God in anguish. Jesus did not say, *"My Father, My Father... "* for we might be too tempted to muse that only the Son of God could endure such agony. No, there is a specific will for every believer, and we all must work through our human feelings of abandonment. The will of God is not at all glamorous; it is extremely lonely and painful.

The powerful but distressing process of agony has been completed in you and me when we have punctuated the will of God; *"It is finished."*

REFLECTIONS...

How has the process of the agony of Jesus impacted your personal view of its importance in your growth. Draw your own parallels with Gethsemane. Are you more empowered by this process, more secure in its usefulness in your development?

Day Three

LOSS

"And the Lord said unto Satan, Behold, all that he hath is in thy power. Only upon himself put not forth thine hand. So Satan went forth from the presence of the Lord." Job 1:12

To suffer loss is to suffer ruin. The story of Job offers us the quintessence of the phenomenon of loss, with its change and result.

Let's trace the process of this great man. His story is a striking tapestry of the condition of human loss, with threads of the sovereignty of God lovingly interwoven.

In the book of Job, we discover that this man was perfect, upright, and reverent of God. He even avoided evil. He was extremely wealthy, in his household and his substance. He was considered the greatest of the east! In verse 4, we conclude that his children were adults because they hosted their own birthday celebrations. Job still had the respect of his children because he called them together after these feasts in order to sanctify them, and offer burnt offerings on their behalf. Imagine calling all of your grown-up children together for an impromptu prayer meeting, and having all of them show up!

Clearly, the first five verses of this book paint a portrait of a powerful man. Job was undoubtedly sought after for advice on business and family affairs.

Contrast this account with verse 12, the point of loss for Job. Satan attributed the excellent attitude of Job to the favor of God. Surely, if Job didn't have this hedge around him, he would display his true colors, and curse God. God grants permission for the attack, with specific instructions, and the process of loss begins. What is missing? We have just learned, in the first five verses, that Job was a great man; the greatest.

He was so personally powerful that he ensured his adult children's relationship with God with annual peradventure prayers. Yet, the institution of Job's loss process was generated without his permission or knowledge.

Picture the heavenly conference room where verse 12 is taking place. Satan is present for the meeting, and God is surely present; but there is no mention that powerful Job has been invited to this tete-a-tete. This is the basis of the devastation of the phenomenon of loss.

Loss is completely out of our personal control. We all strive to gain control. We need to control our lives, our existence, and our environment. We buy nice homes, land great jobs, and build personal kingdoms in hopes of insulating ourselves. When we are forced to suffer loss, it shatters our sense of personal power. We are confronted with a universal truth: God is in supreme control.

We all want to know God as our Savior, because the thought of being saved from something is appealing; but few of us dare to allow loss to cause us to know God as our Lord, the sovereign controller of our lives.

Here, we find our power; even the chaotic process of loss is subject to the authority of God. Satan was only permitted to cause Job as much pain as God allowed. We can be comforted, even in the ruins of loss. God is ever-present in His Holy Conference Room, regulating this process in the lives of you and me, just as He did for Job!

We can turn to Job 13:15 to find the change that this phenomenon is sure to produce.

TRUST
"Though He slay me, yet will I trust in Him: But I will maintain mine own ways before Him." Job 13:15

Trust is twofold: The noun, trust, is the calm state of confidence in the character, strength, and truth of God; the verb, trust, is our permission for God to go, stay or do something without being afraid or anxious about the outcome. So, trust in God is what it is, and what it does.

I had a particularly difficult time with this process, because I could not fully understand trust. I thought of trust as a passive activity done in the face of circumstances over which I had no control. When my daughter died, I heard the voice of the Lord tell me to trust Him with it. Since I could not change the outcome of the events on that day, I did not assign blame to God for her death. But, I now know that trust is not merely the absence of blame when the phenomenon of loss is too great to humanly comprehend. As I began to study the book of Job, I learned that trust is a skill that is developed in stages, and must be accessed through the active participation in the loss process.

As we continue to trace the loss of Job, we find that he has uttered a lofty proclamation. *"...Yet will I trust Him..."* Wow, this Job certainly is a great man if he can manage to muster such resolve after a loss of this magnitude. He has just lost his family, his substance and his health for no apparent reason; but he is still able to decide to trust God.

Job's pledge found in our key verse is the choice of trust; trust must begin in the will of a person. We can only begin to trust God with a solemn decision to do so. But, the book of Job is filled with several cycles of debate and lamentation. It is from one of these cycles that the choice to trust God has been lifted. Even within his change, we find that Job is still protesting the fairness of his situation. Job moves through this book with several bouts of ups and downs, as he begins to learn to trust God. This labyrinth of human emotion can be found in chapters 15-31.

So, what exactly is trust? Trust, in its matured form, is the state of calm confidence in the character, strength, and truth of God which allows us to grant Him permission to go, stay, or do something without being afraid or anxious about the outcome.

What Job is engaging in, as he moves through several chapters of questions, charges, and conclusions is the work of trust. Job needs to find some meaning in the disaster of his process, and God has factored Job's trust timetable into the equation. If you have read the 16 chapters (15-31), you noticed that Job debates with friends, family, and even himself about the reasons for this phenomenon in his life. He has not voided his trust covenant with God; God allowed Job the time he needed to work through his feelings.

The work of trust is vital to us. We need to dispel our imaginations about loss and challenge our perceptions about suffering. We may think that loss is reserved just for sinners or really bad people. We may be pulled into altercations with well-meaning friends who insist on the retributive insinuation of our plight. There, in the tedious work of trust, we begin to slowly unravel our personal tenets about the character, strength, and truth of God.

We can never graduate to the maturity of trust if we remain steeped, a virtual prisoner of our own thinking. We will impede our progress, spending our time submitting and resubmitting our resume to God. We will become indignant, convinced that our Father is causing our considerable dismay.

Let's dare the know the know the strength, character, and truth of our God, so we can give Him our permission to go, stay, or do something without being afraid about the outcome. This will set us on a course towards an exhilarating result.

THE REALITY OF GOD
"I have heard of thee by the hearing of the ear, but now mine eye seeth thee." Job 42:5

Why do we need to complete the process of loss, and unlearn all of our misinformation? We need to clear our consciousness of the cobwebs of religious concepts in order to see God!

Many may think, at first glance, that the result of loss is the restoration of our treasure, as happened to Job in Chapter 42. But, Job lost all he held dear, lamented his pitiful state, toiled tediously in the work of trust in order that he could see God. He even had to receive a powerful tongue lashing from God as his humanity collided with the sovereignty of the Lord (Chapters 38-41).

God is not interested in being a mere sermon topic pronounced from a pulpit, or a vague idea we perceive, or even a fashion statement that fades into time. It matters little to God how intricate the tales of Him have been spun, for this relegates Him to being a rumor.

We have already discovered that Job was the greatest man in the east. He was perfect and upright. He was a man who avoided evil, and revered God; but, heretofore, God was only a rumor to Job.

A rumor is debatable; its validity lies deeply in the oratorical skill of its champion. But seeing God accomplished in Job that which a rumor could not.

Job's rumor caused him to doubt the character, strength, and truth of God. He believes his loss is a punishment from God (13:23), he believes that God is unfair (20:5-7), and he believes that he doesn't deserve this sentence (23:3-5). A rumor has caused dear Job to believe that the pain of loss is not activated in the life of someone who is righteous.

The conventional logic would imply that you must see someone in order to begin to trust him; but Job clearly had to learn to trust God, before he was able to see Him.

Loss burns a trust-sized hole in the soul of a child of God, the bigger the loss, the bigger the hole. This hole is the human capacity to rely on God, eventually becoming confident enough to permit Him to us take down this path or that.

What happened when Job saw God? Job 42:6 gives us the inevitable human reaction to the reality of God: Job repented! God allows the process of loss of personal power, moves us to a place of trust in unexplained power only to cause us to see the very source of power. When we finally see God, in all his love-laced sovereignty, it will bring us to our knees.

The eventual restoration of the household of Job is indeed powerful, but the reality of God that only his loss process could produce remains the greatest miracle in the life of this amazing patriarch.

REFLECTIONS...

After thoroughly reading the powerful testimony of Job, can you begin to embrace the inescapable process of loss that must be completed in your own life? Has God managed to become a reality for you instead of a mere rumor? Compose a love letter to God that explains what your loss process has meant to you, as you now understand it.

Day Four

CHASTISEMENT

"For whom the Lord loveth He chasteneth, and scourgeth every son whom He receiveth." Hebrews 12:6

Chastisement is the correction of the Lord through circumstances. It seems rather difficult to imagine that something unfortunate can befall a child in order to correct some offense, and, more incredibly, this circumstance can emanate from the heart of a loving Father. But, through our careful consideration of the prophet, Jonah, we will draw that very conclusion. The completion of this process is crucial, because the lives of many will rest in our result.

Let us begin to explore the phenomenon of chastisement as recorded in the book of Jonah. Jonah was told by God to go to a city, namely Nineveh, and announce the destruction of the Lord (Jonah 1:1,2). Jonah decided to go to Tarshish instead (verse 3). The Lord sent a storm that troubled the ship (4,5). The other shipmates found Jonah to be the cause of the calamity (8). Jonah knew specifically what he had done to cause the problem (10). The others looked to Jonah for a solution (11). There was only one way to quell the storm (15).

This brief biographical sketch is chock full of valuable information, but we have outlined the seven basic components of the chastisement phenomenon. The first two elements are related in that they offer the precedent of chastisement: the exchange. When God tells us to do something, He always leaves us with a choice. God is a gentleman, and he will respect our choices; but the exchanges we engage in with Him will always determine the situation in which we find ourselves. The third component of this process is that God's sovereignty is always able to find where we have decided to go; we may run from God, but we will never be able to outrun God. Next, we find that chastisement caused Jonah to be conspicuous.

The storm was sent to the entire ship, but only Jonah was caught holding the short straw, as it were. The final three characteristics of this dreaded process are progressive, and only occur sequentially. They are acknowledgement, responsibility, and abandonment. There must be a brave recognition of the offense, a willingness to own our culpability, and an uncompromising desertion of our self-will.

Yes, the process of chastisement is fraught with the love of our Father; however, it is sure and turbulent. We will cause many innocent people unnecessary distress when we engage God in an exchange that ends in a stubborn, "no"

But, a change is coming…

RIGHTEOUSNESS

"Now no chastening for the present seemeth to be joyous, but grievous: nevertheless afterward it yieldeth the peaceable fruit of righteousness unto them which are exercised thereby." Hebrews 12:11

Righteousness is the state of being aligned with what is right. So, contrary to what we have believed, righteousness is a condition that will lead to an action, not an action that will eventually lead us to a righteous state.

In order to understand the initial reluctance of Jonah to journey to Nineveh, we must understand the nation to which he was sent. Nineveh was part of the Assyrian Empire, a notoriously aggressive nation towards Israel. This pagan nation often invaded the homeland of the children of Israel, even seized property. The kings of Nineveh were cruel and ruthless, and Prophet Jonah did not want to go anywhere near this territory. Jonah did not want this race of people saved; so when God ordered him to go and preach there, he decided Tarshish would be a better destination. This act of civil disobedience seemed righteous enough to Jonah. Afterall, why should a trusted servant of the Most High God mingle himself with the like of these Ninevites? Many of us labor under the fallacy that the ministry assignments handed down to us by God will lead us to the pristine pulpits of steepled church houses replete with God-loving Christians needing a jolt of Jesus-talk. God forbid; God sent Reverend Jonah on a crusade, not a revival!

When we read Chapter 2, we find Jonah spending three days and nights within the belly of a great fish. At first glance, I thought this vertebrate purgatory was the chastening rod of God extended to Jonah for correction. But, as I continued to read this chapter, I discovered that this fish has, in fact, saved the drowning prophet! Chapter two is not Jonah's written complaint about the insufferable cruising conditions; he has penned a psalm of thanksgiving.

Verses 2-9 are the introspective reflections of gratitude from a man who has been saved from certain death.

The significance of Jonah 2:10 is best absorbed when seen in light of Jonah 1:13: *"... the men rowed hard to bring it to land..."* The ship was not close enough to shore that Jonah could have simply swam to dry land when he went overboard. But, the fish vomited the prophet up *upon dry land.* The fish accomplished for Jonah what he could not accomplish for himself. Imagine abandoning your self-will, only to drown in the sea. This would not yield a completed process, so the Lord caused Jonah to be swallowed so he could reach dry land.

Do not be disheartened; our key verse only promises righteousness, afterward. Our chastisement process will always include a season of fish-ferry, but it is not a punishment; it is merely transportation to the shores of righteousness.

The principle of righteousness was driven home to me in a personal way a few weeks ago. I was having a nasty disagreement with my husband. I was convinced that I was right, and my husband was, obviously wrong. Clothed in piety, I prayed that God would show my poor husband the error of his ways. God lovingly interrupted my entreaty, "I am right, and both of you are wrong." I had finally gotten the point: God is always right, and righteousness is merely my alignment with God. We find this very righteousness when we contrast Jonah 1:3 with Jonah 3:3. In both verses, Jonah performed an action; he got up from where he was sitting after an exchange with God.

"But Jonah rose up..." Jonah acted **contrary** to the command of God, so any action he performed could not be righteous.

"So Jonah arose..." After chastisement, Jonah performed the same action, now **because** of the command of God. Jonah has finally entered righteousness; his actions are in alignment with the ever-rightness of God.

This alignment leads to his nation-altering result.

THE JUSTICE OF GOD

"Righteousness exalteth a nation: but sin is a reproach to any people." Proverbs 14:34

Jonah's alignment with God caused him to exalt an entire nation! In Chapter 3, we find Evangelist Jonah holding a remarkable one-day soul winning conference. Even the king turned his heart towards the Lord. How did Jonah exalt Nineveh? Well, the pronouncement of the Lord was for the destruction of this nation; and in their present condition, these people had no direct access to God. Because Jonah obeyed God, he was able to raise the rank of this nation. They now had access to the same God who decreed their demise. Because his heart was changed, the king was promoted to priest, and went before God on behalf of the nation (verse 6).

We may think that justice for these pagans would have been destruction. But, look at Chapter 4:11 *"... cannot discern between their right hand and their left... "* The Ninevites were in utter spiritual darkness!

Real justice is simply doing it God's way; and because Jonah administered the orders of the Lord, he caused a nation to be spared. A nation is nothing more than a geographic territory of people. Your community is a nation of sorts. Your church, job, club or school; these are all examples of nations that await your righteousness.

Righteousness is never a state we are in all alone. God will never send us where He will not take us. When God commanded Jonah to "Go" to Nineveh, He was actually inviting him to "Come, let's go" to Nineveh. When Jonah disobeyed His command, he actually refused His invitation.

When we complete the entire process of chastisement, we will truly appreciate the love of God for all of His people. God is so smitten that He will correct us through our circumstances in order to cause our righteousness. Then He will allow us to raise the rank and status of an entire territory of people entrenched in spiritual obscurity.

REFLECTIONS...

As distressing as the chastisement process can be, what encouragement have you received in this lesson? Take time to consider your personal righteousness, do you find yourself consistently aligned with God? Describe a nation that has been exalted because you administered justice.

Day Five

FAITH
"So then faith cometh by hearing, and hearing by the word of God." Romans 10:17

Of all of the processes we have studied this week; this is the most tragic, if not completed.

To study this process, we must reference Hebrews 12:3b. The measure of faith is the capacity of the human heart to believe in God. Without this seed or potential, salvation is impossible (Romans 10:9). So, if we are born with the measure of faith, what does it mean to have faith come by hearing? We can answer this question with a study of the life and times of Father Abraham.

In Genesis 12:1, God spoke to Abram. He told him to leave from where he was, and travel to a land that remained to be seen. In verse 4, Abram departed with his wife and a few relatives.

The process of faith had begun with a word from God. Abram heard the word of the Lord, and with his measure of faith, he began his journey. Faith did not come to Abram when he heard the word of the Lord, because he had this potential from birth. So, what happened when Abram departed after hearing the word of God? Abram's faith began to be *developed* when he heard the word of God. Hearing the word of God begins the developmental process of our faith.

Whenever God requires us to move from certainty to uncertainty, it the beginning of a faith process. God will always appeal to the innate faith measure in us to begin this phenomenon. No one has a greater capacity to believe in God. Our responses to the word of God will determine our personal faith development. Abram could have waited for a distinct destination from God when he received the command. Because he was willing to cooperate with his process, Abram developed into a most faithful Son of God.

A brief scanning of the next ten chapters offers us a view of the powerful faith process of Abram, who became Abraham in 17:5. Abraham made many mistakes over the course of these years, one as soon as Genesis 12:13. Along this journey, Abraham experienced familial strife (chapter 13), war (14), and more than a little marital pain (16-18). He even repeated his mistakes (Genesis 12:13 , Genesis 20). God kept His promise, and Abraham's son , Isaac, was eventually born (Chapter 21:2). Abraham even had to give up his other son, Ishmael, to live in peace with Sarah (21:14).

The process of faith includes many twists and turns that may cause us to have breakdowns with our loved ones. We may even resort to tactics of personal survival that are contrary to the very faith our process is developing. But we mustn't lose heart; we must commit to continue the journey to the land God will show us.

What does the phenomenon of faith produce? We can turn to Genesis 22:8 to continue our pursuit of faith.

HOPE
"And patience, experience; and experience, hope." Romans 5:4

Hebrews 11:1 is a widely known scripture that defines faith; but, for purposes of this study, we will lift the opening clause for our definition of hope.

"Now faith is the substance of things hoped for..." Faith is the essence or the basis of our hope. Hope is not the stab-in-the-dark wish we have believed it to be. Hope is a skill of developed faith, a quality produced in the heart of a man through his experiences. But hope is not made of just any kind our faith; the adjective, now, is crucial to this lesson in faith.

Turn to Genesis 22:1 *"And it came to pass after these things..."* Now is "after these things". Abraham became eligible for hope in Genesis 22 only after he began his faith process in Genesis 12. First, faith is potential; *now faith* is hope.

I became interested in the study of the process of faith when I studied Genesis 22 for a Sunday School lesson on Abraham. Someone said that Abraham had more faith than we do because he was willing to offer his son as a sacrifice. Another classmate piped in that he was sure glad God never required him to do such an unimaginable task. I even thought that since Abraham was the Father of Faith, he could perform commands from God that no other human could be forced to perform. Than God began to show me the fullness of this chapter. God did not require that Abraham offer Isaac as a sacrifice until He had developed Abraham's faith. There would have been a different outcome if God had commanded Abraham to carry out a similar charge in Chapter 12 because faith is progressive. God will never require of your measure of faith that which can only be accomplished by your skill of hope.

In verse 5 of Chapter 22, we find the evidence of the change of developed faith.

Abraham was not merely voicing a wish that he and the lad would go and return again; he spoke the words of a hope produced by the experience of his faith process. Hope caused Abraham to confidently assure his companions that he and Isaac would go yonder, and both he and Isaac would return. But, the change of hope is not completed in Abraham until verse 8 when he proclaims to Isaac that God will provide a sacrifice for Himself. Hope is not hope until it is sure that God will accomplish His will based on the experiences of the faith development.

What resulted from the development of the measure of faith, and the correct allocation of the precious skill of hope in the life of Abraham? We can turn to verse 14 of this chapter to complete this vital process.

THE APPEARANCE OF GOD

" Beloved, now we are the sons of God, and it doth not yet appear what we shall be: but we know that, when he shall appear, we shall be like him: for we shall see him as he is. And every man that have this hope purifieth himself, even as he is pure." 1 John 3:2,3

If ever there was a process that must be completed, it is the process of faith! If we do not allow ourselves to perfect our faith, we cannot see God. At first glance, the power of our key verses may seem to be the promise that we shall be like God, but we must begin to grasp the initial power of the appearance of God. God is definitely going to come back for us, but look closer at the verse.

"...When he shall appear..." What, beyond the coming of God is being promised to us here? Appear means to become tangible evidence of. I was completely bowled over at the powerful result of the faith process. When we participate with the development of our measure of faith and produce the skill of hope, we will be able to have God become tangible evidence to us. God will appear or become visible to our understanding.

Abraham took his son on a journey because he hoped in God. Verse 3 in our key verse tells us that hope causes a man to begin to purify himself. Abraham was not willing to hold anything back from his God, including his promise!

Let's continue our investigation of Abraham, as it relates to our key verses. We have noticed, in Genesis 22:5, that Abraham made a declaration of hope; in verse 8, he sealed his expectancy with the assurance that God would provide for himself. Abraham has taught us a valuable lesson about our attitude in the midst of a faith process. Abraham did not allow himself to commiserate with Isaac about the unfairness of the request by God. Abraham continued to exude hope in God, undoubtedly allaying the concerns of young Isaac.

When we read verse 9, we can see a parallel with 1 John 3:3. Hope has caused Abraham to begin his purification process. It was not the sacrificing of Isaac that evidenced Abraham's hope in God; Abraham refused to mix his commitment to God with anything, even his natural love for his son. What was his hope in? Abraham did not go to the place of sacrifice intending for God to stop him from slaying Isaac. If he had, the voice of the Lord would not have had to call him twice to get his attention (verse 11). No, Abraham's hope was in Gods becoming tangible evidence to him. He had walked with God long enough that he was willing to give up the promise of God for the appearance of God.

God's all-sufficiency became visible to the understanding of Abraham as he lifted up his eyes in verse 13, and saw the ram in the bush. *Finally*, Abraham understood the sovereignty of His God; only God can perform for Himself that which He requests from us. We need not be afraid of the command of God to sacrifice the promise we hold so dear.

A faith process will bring into sight that which a developed experience will expect. Notice in Genesis 22:8, Abraham spoke, with his skill of hope, that God will provide His own sacrifice; in verses 13, he lifted up his eyes and *saw*. Father Abraham saw the very provision his hope had caused him to look for. No wonder he re-named that place (verse 14).

Now, Abraham is a Son of God. We must begin to embrace faith as the progression that it is. Romans 8:14 gives the prerequisite for sonship, and Abraham has allowed himself to be led through his personal faith process in order to be called a Son of God. The appearance of God and the likeness to God are only guaranteed to the Sons of God.

This is crucial to the believer. We must allow our measure of faith to be developed when we hear the word of God, and our experience to produce hope in God, in order that we become a Son of God; because only a son will ever look with expectancy for the appearance of God.

REFLECTIONS...

Reflect on your personal faith process. Consider the many twists and turns you have taken; did you become discouraged and abandon the quest? If so, quickly re-align yourself with your father, and continue on the journey so God can become tangibly evident and visible to you. Chart your growth below.

PURPOSE IN PAIN

"FEAR NOT, LITTLE FLOCK, FOR IT IS YOUR FATHER'S GOOD PLEASURE TO GIVE YOU THE KINGDOM" LUKE 12:32

Day One

OBEDIENCE

"Though He were a Son, yet he learned obedience through the things which he suffered." Hebrews 5:8

Many of us, as mothers, try to teach our children the value of obedience by allowing them to endure unpleasant circumstances. We may feel that a situation will bring our rules closer to the heart of our dear little ones.

I have two small stepchildren who have, just this past week, learned this principle. They love to watch a cartoon video every night after they have taken their baths. This is a ritual that I dare not interrupt; but lately, I started to notice that they were unusually tired before the movie was even half over. This seemed out of character for them, since they would talk all day about the video they would watch at bedtime.

The other day, after I had laid them down for their mid-day nap, I left their room. Instead of going downstairs, as I usually did, I went into my bedroom and listened. Within seconds, the reason for their sleep deprivation was clear. They jumped from their beds, and began to play with their toys. As if used to this kind of surreptitious activity, they were extremely quiet; only an occasional sound emitted from an errant toy, falling to the floor.

There, in my bedroom, I stood amazed; but I decided to take another course of action with the children. I let them continue to fritter away their nap time without making a big deal out of it. I quickly appeared in their doorway, so they knew I was aware of their disobedience. But, I never issued an ultimatum.

That pattern continued for another day or so; the children even invited me into their room to play. I never joined them; I kept my distance to give the impression that I still meant for them to take their required nap.

I never punished them for their behavior, and they still got to get out of bed at the same time. I simply came into their room every day, and roused them from their beds, which they only managed to *sleep* in for approximately 15 minutes per day.

They really began to think they had gotten one over on me, because they still got to watch their treasured videos every night.. But, something interesting happened on the third day, when I began to think that they really had gotten one over on me. They became quite cranky late in the afternoon, and by bedtime, they were fast asleep before their little heads hit the pillow. I never changed their nap schedule, and they still got up at the same time every day, whether they had sufficient rest or not.

This eventually became apparent to them. They actually began to sleep during naps, and video nirvana was restored!

Jesus, the beloved Son of God, came to this earth wrapped in human flesh. He allowed Himself to learn what it means to obey the charge of God, even when that obedience costs incredible suffering. Yes, Jesus felt the pain of obeying His God, but now He is our High-Priest; He understands what it means to have to obey a commandment even when it hurts (Hebrews 4:14). So, when we need to present our petitions to Him, in distressed prayer, He is very deeply touched with our concerns. Still, we must be willing to learn how to obey God, by any means necessary. This is what Jesus' example has taught us to do.

Sometimes, we may find ourselves in painful circumstances, and the only way out is through. We must go through the door of surrendered obedience to our Father. Only then, can we begin to learn what it means to be a child of God. We must never try to compensate God with sacrifice those things which can only be attained through obedience. There really is no other way to learn the precious lessons our dear Jesus learned. May we all end our longing for the shortcuts; may we ever cling to God, and permit Him to teach us the valuable lessons we must learn.

We must learn to obey God inspite of the things we suffer, and by the things we suffer. We will never be able to escape this pain; God has us on a predestined course. We are learning to abandon our foolish devices, lest we be too exhausted to enjoy the very blessings we so desperately desire.

It is time for us to develop obedience to our Father, on His schedule, and by His rules. My stepchildren can attest to the fact of the joy we will experience when we have the energy to savor the happiness He has planned for us.

REFLECTIONS...

Have you ever experienced pain that was so distressing that you thought you could not possibly by expected to obey a command from God? Or, have you ever sensed that obedience to God was the only way out of a personal dilemma?

Read 1 Samuel 4:3. What did the Israelites do in response to loosing a battle against the Philistines? This one act caused them several years of pain (chapter 7:2). What advice did Samuel give to the people to accomplish their deliverance (verse 3)? What is the response of the people (4)?

Day Two

DEPENDENCE

"And he said unto me, My grace is sufficient for thee: for my strength is made perfect in weakness. Most gladly therefore will I rather glory in my infirmities, that the power of Christ may rest in me." 2 Corinthians 12:9

There is a reliance on the Father that can only be fostered within the throes of immense pain. I remember, several years ago, when my five year-old daughter, CoCo, was accidentally killed by a speeding car. In an instant, my whole world collapsed as I watched her lay lifeless in the middle of the street, so close to home. I began to beg God to please spare her life because the alternative thought was too great for my mind to even imagine. The damage to her little body was evident to all that stood in utter terror as she was lifted onto a stretcher, and rushed to the nearest hospital.

I waited the interminable 20 minutes or so until the doctors came to confirm my deepest suspicion: my baby girl had died. I was inconsolable, so purely devastating was the blow.

I began the five-day task of informing loved ones, notifying her school, and arranging her funeral with her father. I also had to continue to care for my three remaining children, two of whom had witnessed the tragedy.

The days followed in a haze of visitors, relatives, and busyness. I simply had to bury my child, as unnatural as it seemed to me.

How I wanted that day, October 29, 1993, to have ended differently. How I longed for my child to have merely sustained minor injuries, anything but this. I couldn't even remember all of the sermons I had heard over the years that would soothe at a time like this. All I could muster, as I peered from the window of the courtesy car sent for me by the hospital, was, "God, please."

Until this time, I thought grace was just the unmerited favor from God in order to accomplish a specific task. But, as I sat by Courtney's bedside holding her still hand, her tiny fingers a silent testament to the horror of the afternoon, grace become an incredible empowerment to me.

I absolutely clung to God during that week. I felt certain I would not be able to endure the entire funeral; surely I'd die. But first, I made it through the processional, than the hymn, than the eulogy, and finally the steady stream of attendees offering heartfelt condolences.

What I now know about grace is that it is also a virtue from God which allows me to operate in a strength or courage that is not my own. It is Heaven's response to the pleading heart that fully fastens itself to the Father in uncompromising dependence.

I cannot promise you that no heart-rending pain will befall you. When it comes, if it hurts so badly that you feel you will die, but you don't; then, my friend, it's grace.

Paul had to learn how to minister both in the unmerited favor of God, and out of the divine virtue of God. He had an issue in his flesh that caused him considerable discomfort, so much that he sought the Lord for its removal.

Perhaps he thought the work of the Lord would be furthered is he did not have to contend with this annoying problem. Maybe he reasoned that the thorn distracted him too much, and its removal would lend credence to his proclaiming the power of God. I am sure his reasons for wanting the situation in his life to be different were well founded, but imagine his surprise when God gave him this answer.

God did not remove the thorn, and Paul had to learn to live with it. Not only live with it, but also become glad. Glad, how can this kind of distress cause anyone to become glad? Paul has discovered the power in the purpose of dependence. The pain in Paul's life caused him to become dependent on God, and his dependence invoked the power of God. There are places in the power of God that are only accessed by the pain of a distressed heart. There is really no other way for the omnipotence of God to be realized outside of the admitted weakness of the human heart. God will not allow His children to harness the power of grace without this vital admission because we may be tempted to suppose that we have developed this virtue with human ingenuity. But imagine Paul's plight; he had to learn how to continue to live the rest of his life out of the favor (kindness) and virtue (strength) of God. The thorn was still firmly in place, but Paul had a course to finish. Dependence on God was no longer a luxury this apostle could exercise at will. Paul *needed* God; his next steps were contingent upon God. He no longer could depend on his own strength to minister, for his strength was flawed. Paul was now forced to dangle on the rope of God's strength, suspended only by God's kindness. At that moment, Paul's weakness collided with God's strength and there really was no match. Now the thorn that caused so much distress was subject to grace; no wonder Paul became glad!

Pain is not God's permission to abandon our ministry. We are still required to fulfill the mandate of heaven, even with discomfort in our flesh. Sufficient grace is available for us all, but this divine power can only be activated by the dependent believer who learns to live with their weaknesses shrouded within the strength of God, and learns to be glad about it.

REFLECTIONS...

Draw a personal parallel between your dependence on God and the grace of God for you. What can you learn about your weaknesses and God's strength?

Read Judges 16. Samson suffered pain that was, in part, his own doing. However, what can we learn about the power of the dependent believer in verses 28-30?

Day Three

FELLOWSHIP
"That I may know him, and the power of his resurrection, and the fellowship of his sufferings, being made conformable unto his death." Philippians 3:10

Many believers are content when they have entered into relationship with God, but there is a place of fellowship with God that is enjoyed when we partake in suffering.

Relationship, the state of being family members, is indeed crucial to the believer; but, fellowship, the state of friendly relationship, allows us to enter intimacy with God. Our relationship makes us connected to God, but our fellowship enables us to enjoy communion with God.

Two years ago, I began to sense the will of God for me to marry. I had learned that marriage, for me, would be incredibly decentralizing. Around that same time, my closest friend shared with me that the man I would eventually marry would be one with whom I had shared a painful history. This seemed like a terribly ominous warning, instead of confirmation of what I had picked up in my own spirit.

Then, I met Michael. Over our two-year courtship, we experienced tremendous pain. Everything that could happen to cause a couple to throw in the towel had happened to us. We are the original unlikely pair, each surviving our own painful pasts. Together, we're learning how to survive our painful history. Okay, so Chareese was right; by the time this book is published, I will be married to my very best friend in the whole world.

Now, I don't spend my time wondering if our marriage will last. We have elected to become members of the same family, but the fellowship of our sufferings has made us a team. I am his most ardent supporter, and he is my eternal hero.

Fellowship is the proving ground for the sufferers; it is where the relationship gets friendly and communal. The work of suffering can be so tedious that it causes us to begin to rely on the intimate fellowship of a vested comrade.

Paul was a man of great intellect; he was considered one of the most learned men of his time. In reading the preceding nine verses of our key text, we find he even had a certain royal lineage. Still his accomplishments had brought Paul to a place of longing; Paul wanted to know his God! We all know God, like we know that two halves equal one whole. But, what Paul is insinuating in this text is that he longs for a knowledge that defies simple cerebral appreciation of established facts. God cannot be learned, or mastered by intellectual pursuit; He must be known, or personally experienced.

Since we are asserting that there is power in the purpose of fellowship, then why are we studying a passage that clearly attributes power to resurrection? Let's look closely at the clause containing our purpose, as it relates to Paul's longing.

"That I may know him...and the fellowship of his sufferings, being made conformable to his death." We can restate this desire with what we now know about fellowship and knowing God. *"That I may personally experience him...and the communion of his sufferings, being made conformable to his death."* Paul wanted to personally participate with Jesus, and he understood that a friendly relationship would be forged between them within the sufferings. But, what good would come of his being made conformable to the death of Jesus? To conform is simply to become like. Paul is, in fact, stating that the way to know Christ is to experience His sufferings, eventually becoming like Christ, death and all. This death would qualify him for the power of the resurrection; you cannot resurrect something that is not dead! The power of resurrection was reserved for Jesus; Paul had no direct access to it. All the things he had gained up to that point (verses 5,6) could not provide him entrance into the knowledge of God. No wonder he counted it loss (8).

Now that Paul has abandoned everything, he is free to enter the community of the fellowship of Christ's sufferings.

The purpose in some of our sufferings when we desire to know Jesus is to make us *like* Jesus, and Jesus died. We must come into alignment with His death process in order to qualify for the power of His resurrection. As painful as this time is, we are in fellowship with Christ; Jesus is our intimate friend!

Dear Lord: Thank you for inviting me to share in this experience with you. Help me not to faint in the middle, rather empower me to continue through this journey with you so that I may know you.

REFLECTIONS...

Compose a personal prayer to the Lord and thank Him for allowing you to share in the special communion that your fellowship in sufferings has brought.

Read Jeremiah 1:5-8. What did God command of Jeremiah? What distress was this child feeling when he uttered verse 6?

Day Four

REVELATION
"For I reckon that the sufferings of this present time are not worthy to be compared with the glory which shall be revealed in us." Romans 8:18

The problem with pain is that it feels like it will never end. We take little comfort when our well-meaning friends promise that it won't last forever. When it hurts, now is the only forever that matters to us. But, be encouraged, it actually came to pass!

I knew a woman who suffered incredible personal pain many years ago. She was a person of tremendous inner beauty, courage, and strength of character. Because she was a minister, her personal trials became open to public opinion. Her turmoil was often gauged throughout the congregation; many parishioners watched to see her varied reactions.

I remember sitting in the pews Sunday after Sunday, wondering if she would finally crack under the strain of open scrutiny. Would the humiliation of the circumstances force this precious woman of faith into hiding, a self-imposed exile to escape the studied glare of the church members?

But, something very different happened. The more pain she endured, the more dynamic her preaching became. Over the course of a year, she developed into one of the most inspiring Bible teachers in our church. It was almost as if the pain in her life served to illuminate the radiance of her spirit; she literally glowed.

Now many years since I have last seen this woman, I still remember her. I remember her powerful preaching, her anointed intercessory prayers, and her undaunted stand for the holiness of God. I am aware of the personal hardships to which she was subjected, but they pale in comparison to the luminance of her spirit and the effectiveness of her ministry.

I met this sister at a time in my life when I sincerely wanted to know God. I had prayed, on several occasions, *"Lord, show me your glory."* The experience of knowing this yielded vessel of God made this possible for me. I thought to myself, as I watched her life, "That must be what God is like."

I was aware of her suffering, but I was impacted by the sheer Godliness that glowed so brilliantly in her. Because of her, I began to look at Romans 8:18 with new interest.

This verse has always given me hope for the promised glory to be revealed in me after the time of suffering. I have always relied on the assurance of my heavenly reward as I have endured the pains of life.

But, after the experience I had many years ago, I began to look at this verse as it relates to the request of Moses in Exodus 33:18. He wanted God to show Himself. Moses wanted to know what God was like. I looked up glory in my concordance to gain some insight for this lesson. Instead of a definition for the word, glory, I found the cross-reference - see 'God'. I found 'glory' listed as a subdivision , 'God/ attributes of'. An attribute is a character trait, something that distinguishes. I nearly fell out of my chair, so explosive this verse became to me!

The sufferings we are subjected to allow the glory or character of God to be revealed *in* us. We all want God to be revealed to us, but we become canvasses for the quality of God to be shone through us. In order to gain an appreciation for what our sufferings are accomplishing; let's restate this verse with our new information.

"For I reckon that the discomfort I am going through now pales in comparison with the character of God that is showing through me, ***at the same time.****"*

What power, there is no longer a need to hang our heads in shame when our private distress becomes public knowledge.

We will be remembered, the trials recalled. But, when the story is re-told, only the glory of God will matter. There are many Moses' in our midst, who go before God in humble query, *"Lord, show me your glory."* God needn't hide these seekers in the rocks to catch a glimpse. We are the manifestations of His glory.

We will lay hold to the power in the pain when our suffering serves as a backdrop for the redolent attributes of God, causing some soul to look on us and conclude, "That must be what God is like."

REFLECTIONS...

Take a moment to consider the request of Moses in Exodus 33:18. Now, compare how that question could be answered to modern-day Moses in looking at your life. What attribute of God do you manifest, what attribute would you like to further cultivate.

Read 2 Corinthians 3:2. You are a letter written of Christ and ministered by your leadership. Below, imagine yourself reading your own letter. What do you think you say about Christ, as ministered by a spiritual teacher or leader?

Day Five

CONSEQUENCE

"For he that soweth to the flesh shall of the flesh reap corruption. But he that soweth to the spirit shall of the spirit shall of the spirit reap everlasting life." Galatians 6:8

We tend to externalize the cause of our pain; someone else must be to blame for our suffering. It might add insult to injury to even consider that some of our plights may, at least in part, be a result of some choice we have made.

One night, as I studied for my Sunday school lesson, I became intrigued with the ludicrous exchange that occurred between Jacob and Esau (Genesis 25:27-34).

You see, Esau wanted a bowl of stew that Jacob, his brother, was preparing. Claiming to be too hungry to need it, he traded his birthright to Jacob for a portion. In those days, the birthright referred to the inheritance rights of the firstborn son. The blessing was pronounced on the son at the time of his father's death.

Here is where it gets ludicrous; why would Esau trade something as inalienable as his birthright for a mere meal? The inheritance was guaranteed to Esau simply because of his birth order so it was intrinsic. To trade it for a bowl of stew was as if trading his very birth order, it was untradable! What Esau did, in effect, was sell the not-yet for the right-now; he traded apples for oranges. This temporary shortsightedness will undoubtedly cost him a dear price, more dear than he realizes at the time of the exchange.

Genesis 25:34 is the basic reason Esau sold his birthright: *"...Esau despised his birthright..."* Esau did not *hate* his birthright; he counted it as worthless. He did not esteem his blessed birth order above what he wanted at the time. It was as if he thought his inheritance would be of little value if he couldn't silence his growling stomach.

Even Jacob realized the value of his brother's birthright. Poor, hungry Esau; he thought he managed to negotiate a pretty nifty deal.

Genesis 27:36 outlines the consequence of the choice that Esau had made. The bitter proclamation of Brother Esau clearly shows the external instinct. He immediately blames his unfortunate position on the wiles of his brother. Could it be that he finally realizes the value of what he has so recklessly given away?

Consequence cannot be revoked when we have sown to the flesh. Reciprocity is a divine law that God has set into nature: we must reap what we sow. We can come to think of pain as a cruel punishment from an insensitive God. Indeed, we can even blame God for the consequence we reap according to the seeds we have sown. We can feel powerless if we consistently believe that another is responsible for our pain.

God is not an uninterested judge sitting on His righteousness, meting out random discomfort for no apparent reason. There is a difference between punishment and consequence. Punishment is penalty; consequence is result. A punishment, used by God, corrects wrongdoing; we have no control over our punishments. Consequence is simply the effect of our own choices; we control our consequences by our personal choices. We can sow, or choose, to the flesh, or we can sow, or choose, to the spirit. The seeds we sow by our choices will ultimately determine the results, or consequences, with which we must live.

In the equation of life, our character is the sum total of our choices; we must consistently sow to the spirit in order to reap the everlasting life we have been promised.

How empowering! I can participate with my result when I make the right choice. I am not some unsuspecting victim of the cunning deceit of a foe. The level of power is amazing when we dare to .sift through the rubble of our condition in order to uncover our role in the pain.

Esau probably would have not felt so powerless had he admitted that Jacob could not have taken what he did not give away.

I continue to learn to esteem my guaranteed birthright above everything, including a temporary desire in my flesh.

Yes, there is power in the pain, even of consequence. We can use our seeds to plant the very harvest we hope to enjoy.

REFLECTIONS...

Reflect on Genesis 25:27-34, 27:30-37. Have you ever relinquished your standing in the family of God for a momentary desire in your flesh? Why do you suppose Esau spoke so bitterly in verse 36?

Read Luke 15:11-16. What consequence did the prodigal son suffer as a result of his actions? What does verse 18 show us about his feeling about his pain?

PROMISE IN PAIN

"The Lord is not slack concerning his promise, as some men count slackness; but is longsuffering to us-ward, not willing that any should perish, but that all should come to repentance." 2 Peter 3:9

Day One

DOMINION WITH GOD

"If we suffer, we shall also reign with him; if we deny him, he also will deny us." 2 Timothy 2:12

My sister once told me a story about a woman she knew. This woman was employed many years ago with a company in its infancy. When the company experienced rapid financial decline, she continued to work, often without commensurate compensation. The woman began to perform other duties, as the need arose, and what began for her as a receptionist position grew into a more administrative capacity.

Then, several years into the company's existence, the profits really started to roll in. The growth was steady and sustained, allowing the corporation to eventually become a leader in its field. The woman remained the receptionist, though she continued to perform other vital functions within the organization. The company began to explore new levels of technological development, and their expansion and progression were assured.

One year, at an annual company event, the owners of the corporation presented the faithful receptionist with a controlling interest; she became a co-owner! She was not just a profit-sharer, as a co-owner, she had the power to make decisions. Her faithfulness in the face of tremendous financial embarrassment had qualified her to become one of the corporate directors within the organization.

When I first heard this story, I thought, "How fortunate. What an amazing climb up the corporate ladder." The woman had no specific training for the position to which she was appointed. Why would seemingly intelligent businessmen entrust an entire division of their corporation to this typist? Well, I started to realize that the actions of this woman during the difficult times showed her level of commitment.

The times when she performed tasks not specifically outlined in her job description displayed her character; she was just the kind of person to whom divisions could be trusted. Although she experienced times of discouragement, times she entertained the idea of job-hunting, she remained with the corporation. She had gained valuable administrative skills, skills that would command a much higher salary if taken to a more established corporation. But, she never quit the company; she did not allow the circumstances to make her give up.

Only a sovereign can truly reign. Here, in this country, we have presidents who we elect to hold an office for a specific length of time. When their time is up, we decide on our next president. But God is sovereign; He cannot be elected, and His reign is not time-specific. Since God super-rules, and is not time-constrained, this promise is especially powerful. We cannot attain this authority; God must appoint it.

Why would God promise the sufferer an eternal reign? I would think that an all-powerful God would prevent suffering, not dangle dominion. But suffering is precisely the kind of on-the-job-interview God uses to select His co-sovereigns. God is always watching; He is looking at us when we are distressed. What kind of sufferer are you? Does the stress of the circumstance cause you to blame God, or do you become embittered when you have been severely hurt? Or do you, like the woman in the story, enhance your skills by learning how to get through a crisis. The season of suffering is also the time of extreme opportunity. We may never get in touch with the creative resources in our spirit if we never have personal trial. There is a precious reservoir of tremendous strength and character that can never be accessed outside of the confines of pain. God has deposited many valiant traits in our innermost being, and we actually need the force of our suffering in order to dig them out.

Every sufferer is more valuable after the pain that before it. There is something special developed in our spirits every time it has been wounded. God cannot afford to give an entire division of sovereignty to just any sufferer. So, He just watches; can He trust you with the pain, so He can appoint you to the reign?

There is nothing wrong with feeling the pain of pain: if it hurts, cry. If you feel discouraged, cry. If there are times you do not understand the calamity, cry. But believe in the promise. There is room in heaven for your wounded heart and damaged soul, but there is no room in the sovereignty of God for a quitter.

REFLECTIONS...

Read Revelations 20:4. Try to imagine yourself enduring such horror. For what did their suffering qualify them?

Outline a time in your life when you suffered tremendous pain. What purpose can you now identify, what promise, implicate?

Day Two

PRESENCE OF GOD
"He shall call upon me, and I will answer him: I will be with him in trouble; I will deliver him, and honour him." Psalms 91:15

Consider the story of Shadrach, Meshach, and Abed-nego (Daniel 3). The place of power for this trio was the presence of God in the fiery furnace. I'm sure they would rather not have been placed in the heated cauldron. Sometimes the power of God is only evident in the pain. God was with the three and Daniel from the very beginning; He caused them to find favor in the sight of the king. Through His abiding presence, the four managed to rise to prominence within the king's service.

But the presence of God was not manifested to the king until he ordered the three be cast into the furnace. In verse 25, the king saw the fourth being with his own eyes. I thought to myself as I read this passage, "Why wasn't the king burned to death when he went near the opening of the heated chamber?" In verse 22, we learn that the guards were killed as they led the boys to their fate. But the king went to the mouth of the blistering cavity, peeked inside to take a closer look, and was not consumed. God caused the king to see, with his own eyes, His presence with the trio. No other guard saw the holy walk, and recounted it to the king; imagine his sentence if he had. But, the king saw for himself that God was with the boys in trouble.

I was further amazed as I continued to read verse 25: *"...walking in the midst of the fire..."* God was with Shadrach, Meshach, and Abed-nego in the furnace, but He did not walk them out of the furnace. The presence of God was so powerful that it caused the boys to walk in the midst of the heat! God, literally, stole their attention; He became more important to the boys than the very real terror of the moment.

This story caused me to look at Psalms 91:15 for the promise that it is. Even a furious king cannot move me to depths of pain that can escape the presence of God, or cause inertia.

God will cause even your troublemaker to see His presence in your pain. He will not be able to obtain a report of your untimely demise; with his own eyes, he will see that you are not required to endure the circumstances all alone. God is ultimately controlling our lives, and if He suffers the fiery furnace, He will be with us in it.

This verse is pregnant with the promise of a loving God. I have a fundamental assurance that when I call upon my Father, He will answer me. In order to understand the answer in its entirety, we must understand the grammar of this verse. The use of a colon after the word, 'him', in the independent clause indicates that what follows the colon amplifies or illustrates what precedes the colon. In other words, *"I will be with him in trouble"* is an illustration of an answer from God. Take comfort in God's presence; if you are still in trouble after you have called upon the name of the Lord, He is with you.

The ascension of the Hebrew boys in the king's court is evidence of God's presence; had He not been with them, they would not have found such favor in the king's sight. But what about the furnace, if God really was really with the boys, would they have even been sentenced to death? No, being a child of God is not a get-out-of-pain-free card. No one is exempt; all must pass the furnace test. There will be times we will be subjected to fiery pain heaped upon us in an effort to hamper our love or devotion to God.

God does not show up for us in trouble, He is there all of the time (Matthew 28:20). God has promised to be with us *even* in trouble; trouble does not make God run off and hide. The connotation of God's promise indicates behavior as well as support; God is with us, to be sure, but how He is with us reveals His character. The king spotted the four walking: God is panic-proof! We can count on His unflappable presence.

REFLECTIONS...

Compare Daniel 3:25 with Psalms 16:11. What can we expect to happen to us when we experience the presence of God, even in our pain?

Read Joshua 1:5-9 carefully. God gave several instructions to Joshua concerning the next phase of the Promise. Make a short list of the instructions and commands, and list the one promise God has made to His people?

Day Three

PARTNERSHIP WITH GOD

"But rejoice, inasmuch as ye are partakers of Christ's suffering; that, when his glory shall be revealed, ye may be glad also with exceeding joy." 1 Peter 4:13

Imagine you want to open your own business. You begin to research the merits of your enterprise, and evaluate the possible pitfalls. You find that you will need a partner in order to make a successful attempt at your plan.

A partner is someone who takes on the risks of your endeavor with you, and enjoys the privileges associated with your business. You become bound to the individual, no matter the outcome. A contract links the two of you; you cannot arbitrarily abandon the quest.

Sounds a bit scary when you consider all of the risks involved in partnership, doesn't it? You become accountable to someone; partnership precludes your total independence.

God has been kind enough to drive this particular lesson home to me in a very personal way. There are some advantages to the idea of partnership: you are not alone! There is someone else who is as invested in the success of your venture as you are. Gone are the endless nights of sleepless worry and indecision. The common goals unite the partners.

A partnership is not a random undertaking; you can choose with whom you will partner. Take as much time as you need to review all the terms of the contract, interview all prospects, and interact with your partner.

Finally, in order for a partnership to be possible, there must be a meeting of the minds. You and your partner must share the same vision. Implicitly, within the corporate mindset, is equity of power. Partnership with divergent ideas, and an imbalance of power will serve to eventually frustrate the corporate structure.

Partnership is presence that participates! It is not at all passive. Yesterday we explored the promise of the presence of God; today, we will discuss the promotion to partnership in pain. Partnership is specific; you will be picked out before you will be picked on.

The whole chapter (1Peter 4) is a written contract outlined for the prospective partner. The terms and conditions are set forth. Verse 1 begins with an admonition for the would-be partner; suffering is an inescapable condition of the human existence. If there were anyone who would have been eligible to avoid pain, it would have been Christ. If He, in His flesh, suffered pain, we all will feel distress. As grim as this information may be, verse 1 is also our place of empowerment.

"Arm yourselves... with the same mind." There must be a meeting of the minds. Within this partnership, there is ammunition. When we arm ourselves, we load ourselves with ammunition. This verse cannot be commanding us to load ourselves with the mind of suffering; if we live this life, we will suffer. Which mind is available to the partners of Christ? The mind of Christ! The mind of Christ is crucial to the sufferer who has elected to enter into partnership with Christ; if you do what Christ did, you will get what Christ got (Hebrews 1:3)! How are you loaded? If you find yourself in a painful situation, and you reason, "Oh well, this is just how things are for me," then you have loaded yourself with the wrong ammunition. The mind of Christ offers us insulation when we must go through suffering. We are comforted because we are under contract; Jesus becomes invested in our survival. We cannot have our own way, but we are not forced to figure the outcome all alone. With the mind of Christ, pain looses its ability to cause insomnia; dust off those pillows!

No wonder verse 13 admonishes us to rejoice; the same glory to be displayed so brightly in Jesus will be apparent in each partner! Imagine when Jesus' splendor and majesty is revealed, and it is shone in us.

Read our key verse very carefully: *"... inasmuch as ye are partakers..."* The glory is proportional; we can only reflect the magnificence of Christ *to the degree* that we have been partakers of His suffering. If you decide to sign into a limited partnership, then you will reveal limited glory. Oh, my friend, hasten to become a full-fledged partner with Jesus.

Take full advantage of the call to partnership. Keep the mind of Christ, share His vision, and enjoy His power!

REFLECTIONS...

I am especially encouraged about the promise of partnership in pain. Does this lesson give you a different prospective about some distress you are encountering?

Read 1 Peter 4 in its entirety. Draw up a personal contract agreement with God for partnership. Include some terms and conditions as mentioned in this chapter. What concrete ways can you think of to help you consistently arm yourself with the mind of Christ? Commit yourself to these, and mention them to God.

Day Four

PROVISION OF GOD

"Thou preparest a table before in the presence of mine enemies: thou anointest my head with oil; my cup runneth over." Psalms 23:5

Read Psalms 23. We have finite minds, so we can skip the promise of the provision of God in verse 5. The provision of God is supremely divine.

This piece is a dissertation offered by David. It begins with an essential assertion. The body of this essay serves to support the fundamental truth set forth in the contention, and the conclusion is a logical consequence, given the preceding information.

Now, let's re-read Psalms 23. Verse 1 is the author's essential assertion; it establishes the Lordship of Jesus. This declaration is not David's campaign speech for Jesus to become the Lord: Jesus is Lord! David has discovered something important about himself in the penning of this account. In 1 Samuel 16:19, David is a shepherd, he is in charge of tending the sheep. As a shepherd, he knows the nature of sheep is one of timidity and utter dependence. Yet it is not mentioned that David feels a sense of anger that he has been demoted. He has lived long enough and experienced enough in his walk with Jesus, that he has been moved to admit, *"The Lord is my shepherd..."* As we continue to the second clause, we see another assertion, *"...I shall not want."* Could this be another contention in the dissertation? No, David is not saying that the Lord is his shepherd, *and* he shall not want. David is confessing that *because* the Lord is his shepherd, he shall not want. There is a difference between *posture* and *position*. A position is an arrangement of a sequence, or its parts, posture is the significance of a *particular* part in the arrangement to the entire sequence. Jesus hold more than one position, but His posture remains the same.

Brother David is entering into agreement with a universal truth, and taking comfort in its implication. Because the eternal posture of Jesus, Lord, has positioned itself in front of David as a shepherd, or caretaker, he will not be without anything he needs.

Verses 2-5 all serve to support David's assertion. *"He maketh…He leadeth…He restoreth…"* Because the Lord is in charge of David's care, He is initiating the journey. David, now comfortable in his role of sheep, is following the leader. Well, that is proof of the Lordship of Jesus, but what about the last clause of verse one; how are verses 2-5 supporting the assertion that these acts of leadership are meeting David's needs?

David has not recorded in verse two that he is tired, and then he is made to lie down in green pastures. Because the sovereignty of the Lord includes green pastures, and the providential shepherd has caused David to lie down; he has not become tired.

The cadence of this text has been interrupted in verse 4. Seemingly, the posture and the position of Jesus have been temporarily suspended and poor David has wandered into the valley of the shadow of death. There is none of the divine initiation we have read in the previous verses; there's no, "He maketh me to walk through the valley of the shadow of death." Verse 4 looks more like a parenthetical interjection than evidence of the Lordship of Jesus. Could it be; did Jesus blink and David wandered, as any sheep would, into the dreaded valley? Look closely at verse 4 as it relates to the final clause in verse 3: the valley the shadow of death is *in* the paths of righteousness! What David is proclaiming is that even though the journey has included a jaunt through this valley, he is not afraid. Why, because the Lord is his shepherd!

Now, we see the position of Jesus has changed, *"…for thou art with me…"* The valley where death casts a shadow has caused a re-arrangement.

Jesus is not longer in front of David leading the way as we read in the earlier verses. Now, He is *with* David, indicating that trouble has moved Jesus next to His sheep. Although the position has changed, Jesus is still Lord. Something very subtle has also happened in this painful verse. In the preceding verses, David is speaking to his audience reporting on the Lordship of Jesus; but here we see the author's choice of pronouns has changed; David begins to speak directly to Jesus.

The journey will always include the valley of the shadow of death; it will never consist of the valley. Jesus led David *through* the valley, not *to* the valley.

Verse 5 is our place of promise for this lesson. The presence of enemies has not caused Jesus to hurriedly prepare a table, as if He is a flustered housewife caught off-guard with unexpected guests. No, the table was already prepared. David had to go through the valley in order to get there. Because the Lord is David's shepherd, the preparations were made ahead of time. The presence of the enemies is incidental. You will still get your provision, *even* in the presence of enemies.

Right in the paths of righteousness, deep in the valley of the shadow of death…there's a party going on!

No wonder the conclusion is drawn, *"Surely…"* After a trip like that, the Lordship of Jesus is irrefutable!

REFLECTIONS...

Did this lesson help you view your role as a sheep in a different way? What can you count on for your times of discomfort, because the Lord is your shepherd?

We have seen that the how powerful the position and the posture of Jesus is in our lives. Can you recall a time when you suffered a need because you did not allow the Lord to be your shepherd?

Day Five

COMPASSION FROM GOD

"Therefore, behold, I will allure her, and bring her into the wilderness, and speak comfortably unto her." Hosea 2:14

The story of Hosea and Gomer continues to confound and astonish me, even years after I first read this allegorical account.

Why in the world would a prophet of God, such as Hosea, marry a woman of such questionable character like Gomer? Surely in his illustrious career, which spanned more than 40 years, he had many opportunities to meet a woman more suited to his ministry. Perhaps a nice village girl, or a daughter of one his preacher friends, anyone but Gomer.

In Chapter 1, God told Hosea to marry a wife of whoredoms (verse 2), but Hosea specifically chose Gomer. If God had brought Gomer to Hosea's front door, and commanded him to marry her in particular, then Hosea would not have had any attachment to the marriage. But because Hosea chose Gomer, he shows a personal investment in the marriage: Hosea wants Gomer!

We would all agree that Hosea was a great man of God, but I want us to consider our lesson today from the perspective of Gomer. She was a woman of ill repute, to be sure, but the promise of compassion is one especially for her.

There is a profound sense of loneliness in sin. When we are out of touch with the love of our Father, choosing to live in lawlessness, we begin to experience the very baseness of pain. We can turn our hurt inward for sin saps our ability to relate, even with ourselves. We begin to suffer the devastation of our own bitter recriminations, "Why, oh why, did I allow myself to become entangled in this mess?"

Well, Gomer probably didn't even know how to receive the selfless love of Hosea. She was uncomfortable with such unconditional acceptance.

In her line of work, she needed to maintain some sort of detachment in order to carry out her duties. For her, copulation was commerce, and her marriage to Hosea represented long-term employment. Perhaps she reasoned that Hosea wanted some children or female companionship when he was not out preaching. She could never imagine that this man, Hosea, wanted her. *"This will never work"*, became her perpetual lullaby. Hosea was a well-known prophet of his time. This fact undoubtedly sent Gomer in an emotional tailspin, especially in light of her own seedy resume. I can almost hear this woman's pitiful lamentation as she resorted to the only life she has ever known, as sordid as it was. But Hosea knew God, he knew about the all-consuming love of his Father. He had received this mercy that renewed itself every morning. So, because he had known this kind of love, he chose to invest it in his wife; he still wanted Gomer.

Gomer, despite her shortcomings, had impacted her husband. Verse 2 of Chapter 2 tells us that Gomer was no longer married to Hosea for she had deserted him. He was finally rid of her! Now he was free to find himself another wife, one who could make a real contribution to his ministry, right? But look at what Hosea does; he begins to plead with her children, "Talk to that mother of yours, guys, because she has walked out of this marriage. Now, if she will only give up that futile habit of, you know, we can work this mess out." Hosea still wants Gomer!

Then, Hosea begins to reveal his retribution (verses 3-13). "Tick-tock, Miss Gomer, your time is almost up. I am planning a systematic strike against you. You would not listen to reason; you even dismissed the kids' efforts to make you return to me. Well, Missy, your reign of pain is coming to a swift end. You have no idea what a dangerous game you are playing. I will cause you immense embarrassment; even the lovers you have abandoned me for will desert you. The devices you have used in your endless schemes and wicked perversions will all backfire. I can do that, you know."

We all love a story where the villain gets what's coming to her, so by the time we get to verse 14, we may imagine 101 ways that Hosea can right this terrible wrong done to him by Gomer. We may even cheer him on; Gomer is really a poor excuse for a wife anyway, "Hey-ho, Gomer you've got to go!"

"*...And speak comfortably to her...*" Wait! You mean Hosea is not going to bring this trollop into the wilderness so there can be no witnesses to the murder? Why in the world would he even waste his time going after such an unsavory character as Gomer: Hosea still wants Gomer!

Compassion is come-passion. A passion is a compulsion or urge towards a thing that defies reason; it makes no sense. God is ever moved with come-passion.

Even those times we desert our covenant in favor of selfish pursuits; He keeps coming towards us. When all of our schemes fail, and our foolhardy choices have wrought unspeakable suffering and distress; God will woo into a wilderness, a place to be utterly alone in His presence. There, He will meet us and speak comfortably to us, for God still wants us!

REFLECTIONS...

Compare Jeremiah 30:11-15 with Lamentations 3:32. Why was this nation suffering? What did the prophet come to learn about God in the latter passage?

Imagine your own pain when you have made bad choices. See yourself in your wilderness experience, totally alone with God. He has now spoken comfortably to you (Isaiah 1:18). Record the things you must present to God in humble apology for your desertion. Keep writing until you sense His come-passion.

POWER IN PAIN

"The Lord is my strength, and he will make my feet like hinds' feet, and he will make me to walk upon mine high places." Habakkuk 3:19

Day One

CHOICE

"I will bless the Lord at all times: his praise shall continually be in my mouth." Psalms 34:1

Let's look at 1 Samuel 21:10-15. Here, we find Brother David in a particularly painful time in his life. He is on the run from Saul, who is seeking to do him harm. Now, David finds himself in Gath where the officers of the king begin to recognize him (verses 10,11). Since David overhears the conversation, he fears that his identity will become known, so he begins to pretend that he is insane with offbeat behaviors (12,13). Even though the king refuses to allow David to become his guest after this display, David's performance spares his life (14,15).

This seems like an odd sequence of events to explore in studying the power of choice in pain. While David has gone down in Bible history as being a great king, one after God's own heart, this powerful psalm was penned when he was in the midst of terrible distress. David will bless the Lord at all times, even when he is embroiled in this desperate flight for life. Yes, you have read right; David has not resolved to bless the Lord at all times when his times are favorable and pleasant, this fugitive of injustice has declared his intent while living life on the lam.

We have touched on the power of choice in making life decisions; we can sow our way into everlasting life. Now, we can delve deeper into the power of choice in pain.

Let's review why this proclamation is so empowering. David was special assistant to King Saul, and deeply loved and respected his mentor. There was even a bond between David and Prince Jonathon. But something happened; Saul became extremely annoyed with David because the people began to speak well of David. So, Saul began to devise a plan to eliminate his imagined foe.

David was forced to flee from his murderous mentor. You can find a more detailed account of this brief summation in 1 Samuel 18-20. By the time we find David in Chapter 21, he is well into this escape. If you read the first nine verses of this chapter, you saw that dear David is lying in order to obtain a weapon, obviously for his personal protection. So, David, who loves and respects King Saul, is literally running for his life. Imagine the inner turmoil he must be feeling as he flees from the royal family, from his father figure, Saul; his soul brother, Jonathon; and his wife, Michal. He was forced to leave all he had held dear for much of his adult life. What does David do, when he feels this deep pain? Verse 13 is David's place of power: he changed his behavior!

Why is choice our power in pain? We are all God-created, God-owned beings; we do not belong to ourselves. Contrary to popular opinion, we are not the captains of our own destiny. Still, God has created each of us with a free will. The only thing we completely own is our wills. Psalms 24:1 reminds us that God owns everything else, we are mere stewards. Our choices are the selections of our individual wills. Since God respects His own design, He considers the wills of all of His children. He will not force us to choose anything because the power of choice must emanate from our personal power centers: our wills.

How can we bless the Lord? Well, when God blesses us, it means so much because He gives to us out of the storehouse of His ownership. You can only truly bless the Lord if you give Him something from what you already own; a blessing is not a blessing if you are not the owner. We have already discovered what a colon indicates. David vows to bless the Lord at all times, and what follows illustrates *how* he plans to accomplish this. This key verse also denotes the second basis of a blessing; a blessing is the original idea of the owner. Psalms 34:1 was not written in submissive response to a request of God.

David has *decided* to bless the Lord, because he wants to, and from his ownership. How can he accomplish this when he is a steward over most everything? The thing David can offer to his God is his praise, or his approval. God helped me understand praise when I was writing this section. When you gain approval, it is an effectual, "Yes." Imagine applying for a car loan or home mortgage. When you receive the written decision of the lenders, the letter will invariably begin with well wishes and salutations. We generally skip this portion, scanning the correspondence for the answer to the credit request; is the loan approved or denied? We appreciate the creditor's comments about our character and thanks for our application, but what we are seeking is their approval. While we may think that praise is merely an extended period of cheers, hurrahs, and heartfelt thanks, we have not completed praise if we still have not given God our approval; tell God, "Yes."

What David has concluded, when he is faced with possible death, and the loss of a treasured friendship, is that he will bestow a blessing upon the Lord by giving Him his approval without interruption. David still says, "Yes."

You are empowered in pain when you choose to give the Lord your uninterrupted approval.

REFLECTIONS...

Using the knowledge you now have about the power of choice, please read Hebrews 11:24,25. Describe why this choice made Moses a hero of faith?

Look at Deuteronomy 30:15-20. Here lies the essence of the power of choice. What choices are given to us in this passage, what commandments? From reading this passage, what can you infer will ultimately follow the choice of a person?

Day Two

NEED

"But my God shall supply all your need according to his riches in glory by Christ Jesus." Philippians 4:19

Recently, I began to appreciate the true power of need in my pain. For years, I felt that my need was an indication of my weaknesses and had tried hard to conceal or even avoid this condition. But the closer I got to God in prayer, the more I started to understand the significance of need.

I can best describe how I have come to grasp this power by relating a principle I first learned in a micro-economics class in college. We studied that in order for a company to determine how much of a particular product to manufacture, it must first draw a conclusion about the community need for the product. This principle is known as the law of supply and demand. Simply put, mass production of any supply without a specific demand will cause a corporation to suffer extensive monetary damage; eventually a business will fail with this haphazard tactic.

When I looked in my dictionary to find a definition for need in preparing this lesson, I was startled to find the word, 'demand' listed among its synonyms. This, coupled with what I learned at the feet of Jesus, gave me a new perspective on how powerful a need is. Just as a consumer can operate the faucet of the corporate production valve, we can invoke the divine supply of God simply by having a need.

We learned in our previous lesson that the blessings of God are His choices that flow from His will. They are not divine responses to our requests; they are His idea. God's blessings are without restrictions; they overflow into our beings. These gifts from our Father are too enormous to be contained in our human capacity; we simply do not have room for the magnitude of the blessed gifts of God.

So supernatural, these gifts personify and must make room for us (Proverbs 18:16).

A supply is a different level of giving from the heart of God. A supply is a response. Paul promises that God will supply a need, which means that the need is the power that effects the supply of God. You *must* have a need in order to activate the supply valve.

So, the need that I desired to conceal or avoid actually caused me to become closer to God. How? Well, my need actually caused God to come closer to me. You see, a need is a force that draws the soul towards the supply of God, and this exertion also pulls God closer to us.

Let's look closer at our key verse. *"God will supply all of our need according to His riches in glory"*- where is glory? If we fail to define the place of glory, this verse may seem like a disclaimer for the supplier; God will supply all of our need, while supplies last in glory. Earlier, we learned that glory is an attribute of God. So, 'glory' is located within God, it is part of His personal character. God could not trust something as important as your need to anything else, so He swore by Himself. God will supply all of your need, according to His riches in Himself, and God is more than enough!

But let's dig a little deeper into our powerful state of need. Like our wills, we all have a distinctive, innate need-base. Our individual needs originate in our particular need-base; every need is specific. Let's imagine you need a new home. When you pray, you recognize your need from your need-base and you begin to pray for a home. God supplies your new home, you thank Him, and all is well. But let's consider the intricacy of what has actually happened. Notice our key verse describes 'need' as singular; could this possibly be a typographical error? You and I can attest that we certainly have more than one need, or do we? Look at Acts 17:28; this is clear and convincing evidence of the entirety of the need of man. We need God!

While we identify our need as something tangible, as a home, our need-base is actually seeking more of God. Just like the need-base is in you, the supply valve is in God.

When you experience need, the force of it pulls you towards the supply valve inside God. In James 4:8, this principle is described. Your need draws you closer to God's supply that is inside God, and *that* action draws God closer to you via His supply. In other words, every supply of God is a piece of God given from inside of God.

God is our central need, and God is our eternal supplier. Which means every supply will always fit every need. God does not bless into a vacuum, but He will always supply into the vacuum created by our specific need. Since the promise is that God will supply all our need, the supply valve is not de-activated until the entire need has been supplied. Because God is the ultimate businessman, He will not continue the supply once the need has been met, and He will not supply you with something that is ill fitted to your need. Every need is supply-shaped, and every need that will ever be met will be met with a supply that resembles the supplier. So, enjoy your home, your car, your food; God has moved closer to you through that supply.

We now have a reason to embrace our need. It is so powerful because it causes us to become closer to the supply valve of God, which is *in Him*. There is no other way to access the glory of God, except we need Him.

REFLECTIONS...

Now that we have discovered the power of our need, what do you think about the needs in your life? How do you now view the supplies in your life, now that you are aware of their source? Jot your thoughts.

Read Luke 12:29-31. Here, Jesus explains that He already knows that we have certain needs. With what we know about His promise, what do you suppose He is going to do with the knowledge that we have a certain need? With the time you save not worrying about these needs, what are you charged to do?

Day Three

AGREEMENT

"And I will give unto thee keys of the kingdom of heaven: and whatsoever thou shalt bind on earth shall be bound in heaven: and whatsoever thou shalt loose on earth shall be loosed in heaven." Matthew 16:19

Let's turn to Genesis 11:4-6. Here, we find mankind determined to build a city and a tower to reach up to heaven. They decided to make a monument to themselves, and they thought this construction would make a name for them. In verse 5, the Lord began to survey the progress of mankind and He concluded, *"The people is one"*, in verse 6. Since I majored in English in college, this comment struck me as grammatically incorrect. The subject-verb pattern was inconsistent: the subject, 'people' (plural) did not match the predicate, 'is' (singular). But this passage drove home an important truth about the power of agreement; agreement will cause a group to become one. The plural become singular when there is unity.

I like to think of agreement as group harmony, the collective gathering around a concept. When you enter agreement, the whole becomes more significant than any one of its parts separately. As with our scripture, we must believe that we are most powerful when we can, as a group, gather around a concept. Mankind agreed to build a tower to reach heaven, and we can look at verse 6 to see the result of such unity. *"...And now nothing will be restrained from them..."* The place of power for this group was in verse 4, when they proclaimed, *"Let us..."* This agreement caused God to conclude that, unless He intervened, they would surely succeed with their ill-conceived imagination.

In studying for this lesson, I discovered something powerful about agreement. Look at Genesis 11:7, *"Let us..."* God even agreed with Himself in order to troubleshoot the problems posed by the construction efforts of mankind.

We see another powerful example of God in concert with Himself in Genesis 1:26, and from that agreement, mankind was created.

How can I agree with myself? Well, I reach a place of power when I can achieve congruence between what I tell the world and what I tell myself. For instance, you will live in a perpetual state of internal powerlessness when you vehemently pronounce Biblical tenets as the undiluted truths of God, yet transgress His law in private, unassuming ways. "I believe that thou shalt not steal; but, I can only pay a portion of my required tithe this week." You spend years circling financial impotence until you agree with yourself; gather around the concept that a tithe belongs to God, commit to pay Him what you owe, and watch the power you begin to enjoy.

Let's look closer at our key verse; what caused Jesus to present Peter with keys to the kingdom? Look at verse 16 of the same chapter, *"Thou art the Christ"* Peter entered into agreement with the reality of who Jesus really was. To agree means to admit. Jesus was not asking Peter who He was because He was in the midst of an identity crisis; Jesus was inviting Peter to gather around the truth about who He was, and make an admission of this reality. This confession qualified Brother Peter to handle the keys to the kingdom of heaven because his admission proved that Peter would gather around the truthful concepts that God would reveal to him. God will not entrust the keys to the kingdom of heaven to anyone who is not in agreement with Him. These keys will provide you entrance into an agreement relationship with heaven; God is obligating Himself to work *with* you! This is of vital importance because this understanding will keep you from haphazardly binding and loosing, frustrated by the lack of power.

The kingdom of heaven is anywhere the will of God is being done. You can invite the kingdom when you simply agree that His will is to be done on earth, as it is being done in heaven (Matthew 6:10).

This primary agreement will qualify you to handle the keys of the kingdom of heaven, a means of entrance and source of understanding. God is not going to hand over to you these dynamic keys so you can bind an unfavorable supervisor or loose a new Mercedes. When you invite the kingdom of heaven, you agree that the will of God is to be done. That is why God will enter agreement with you to bind or loose anything that impedes the accomplishment of His will.

Gather around the concept that God is always right, and agree with Him every step of the way. You do not need to build your way to heaven; you can agree with God and invite the kingdom of heaven right where you are, and God will *give* you the keys to unlock its powers!

REFLECTIONS...

Read Joshua 24:15 and Matthew 12:25. Now that we know that agreement is the place of power, why do you suppose it is important to include your house in your declaration to serve the Lord? What will befall a house that has not entered into an agreement as described in Matthew 12:25.

Think about what it means to gather around a concept and agree with God. Write a letter to God in which you invite the kingdom of heaven in your part of the earth; include an agreement with yourself to gather around whatever it takes to complete the will of God.

Day Four

INFLUENCE
"If ye shall ask any thing in my name, I will do it."
John 14:14

Let's look at 2 Kings 20:1-6 for our study today about the power of influence available to us in our pain. King Hezekiah received a visit from Prophet Isaiah, warning him about his impending death. The king prayed to God, pleading for his life. The Lord heard the lament of the king and extended his years. Wow, this king was able access the power of influence in his hour of infirmity.

I readily concede that there is great power in prayer, and King Hezekiah turned his face to the wall and squeezed the power pump of prayer. Anyone would do the same thing if faced with this inevitability, but there is another level of power we can enter when we are suffering pain. Every one is not entitled to exercise the power of influence; this is a special ability reserved for the hurting children of God. God is our concerned Father, and He is always listening to the cries of His children.

King Hezekiah has given us a glimpse into the heart of God towards His children. In verse 5, God assures, *"I have heard thy prayers. I have seen thy tears..."* If we take comfort in these words, then the next promise is also ours to rely on, *"...I will heal thee..."* God is moved with compassion! But, what has precedes the compassion from God? In verse 3, we see that the king recounts several reasons that the Lord should show mercy upon him. But look at the final sentence of this verse, *"And Hezekiah wept sore."*- Hezekiah's heart was broken. More than the impassioned rhetoric, designed to manipulate the sovereignty of God, the broken heart of this king was what ultimately invoked the compassion of God (Psalms 51:17).

The heart of a man is the level field of influence; if elocution was the basis of this power, then only certain people could experience this response from the Lord. While I am deeply impressed with the laudable accomplishments of King Hezekiah, and applaud his efforts to live this kind of life; God was only impacted by his broken heart, and shed tears.

In our key verse, we are promised that if we ask anything in the name of Jesus, He will do it. This sounds simple enough, but look at verse 12 of this same chapter. Verses 13,14 are continuations of the main idea of this text, *"...He that believeth on me..."* We are all born with the capacity to believe in Jesus, but we must choose to actually believe. Jesus says that the soul that will believe on Him will have access to the power of influence as described in our verse. Why, because there is something that happens in the heart of a person who dares to believe God. This verse is not a blank check promise for just any person who wants to engage in a wish list thought life. God is not Santa Claus; the power of influence can only flow from the heart that has been impacted by a determined belief in God. Dare not attempt to exercise the power of influence from an unbelieving heart; you will be woefully disappointed.

Only a fully persuaded heart can ask anything in the name of Jesus, and He will do it, because, just as with King Hezekiah, God will only hear the prayers and see the tears of the broken heart.

REFLECTIONS...

Read Esther 4:11 and 5:1,2. Here we see Queen Esther making a decision to go before the king when it could have cost her a dear price (verse 11). Describe what the power of influence meant to this blessed queen?

Think about the power of influence versus the tactic of manipulation when impacting the heart of God. Are you a child of God who has access to the power of influence in your pain; have you been persuaded to believe in God? Note what it means to you to learn that the heart of the sufferer is the field of influence rather than oratorical skills. Does this affect the way you feel about your attitude in prayer, as well as the words you choose in prayer?

Day Five

REPENTANCE

"When they heard these things, they held their peace, and glorified God, saying, then hath God also to the Gentiles granted repentance unto life." Acts 11:18

Turn to 2 Corinthians 7:10, *"for godly sorrow worketh repentance..."* Repentance means to change your mind, and then your direction. It moves beyond a sorry feeling that accompanies the guilt of wrongdoing. Here, in Corinthians, we find that Paul has written a letter to the church at Corinth, and has assured them that their God-induced sorrow will work in them the stimulation to turn from their sin, and go in another direction. Repentance is not an act that originates in the will of a man; rather it is a result of the gentle prodding of God. God must initiate this power, and only God can grant this opportunity.

Repentance is the power afforded to the believer to begin the arduous process of personal change; it is the foundation upon which all the choices that lead to eternal life are built. Because we are mostly independent thinkers, we tend to suppose that we can repent from our own volition. Repentance is then reduced to a mental whim subject to the mood of the repentant. We can be tempted to thoughtlessly rip open the package of our supposed sorrow, and mindlessly attach it to the wound of our sin. One needs to only look at Romans 6:23 to learn the true cost of sin; there must be more involved in its absolution than a simple, "Oops."

Sin causes such devastation to the human soul that the power to turn from this self-destruction has got to be divine. Look at Psalms 51:5; the psalmist is not recalling that he is a child who was molded into a sinful state because of bad parenting, or conceived into sin because of an isolated act of his mother. This is an admission that sin is not what we do; it is what we are born into, who we are.

After the original salvation experience, there must be a continual commitment to change in order to overcome our natal state. This commitment must originate supernaturally, because we are not born with this ability.

If we read the two verses preceding our key verse, we see that Paul has written this letter to chasten them. Because he really loves these people, he admits to a twinge of regret at their sorrow (verse 9). But he explains that the pain they have experienced is going to provide an inner incentive to turn from their natural inclinations and take the necessary steps towards lasting change. Paul has realized that only this reformation will prepare these Christians eternal life, something that is impossible without repentance. We must never take for granted the power to repent of our sinful ways and tendencies. Without it, we would surely sin our way to death.

Have you been experiencing the sorrow that results for the loving conviction of your concerned Father, and have you been distressed because of it? God really does love us more that can ever imagine; He is using this pain to activate the power of repentance. Then, we can experience a change of mind and direction, and cooperate with His spirit in order to begin to walk in the way that leads to eternal life.

It is God who grants repentance, and He is committed to exhaust all of our discomfort, suffering, and pain in order to energize in us the power to abandon deadly pursuits.

So, when you find yourself in the favor of God to repent, quickly turn; God has given you His permission to change.

REFLECTIONS...

Ponder the generosity of God to grant you repentance so your natural state will not cause your death. Write a thank-you note to our Father, and thank Him for using the pain to cause you to change your mind.

Read Psalms 51. This is a prayer of repentance of David when his sin was exposed to him. List the requests this sorrow caused him to make to God. What are we capable of doing when our hearts have accessed the power to repent unto life (verse 13)?

ABOUT IN MY HEART, MINISTRIES

IN MY HEART, MINISTRIES is a non-profit organization dedicated to the economic, emotional, and spiritual empowerment of women. We **envision** the eradication of the public welfare system, as we know it. Our **mission** is to use our time, talent, and treasure to mend the fractured family, for we believe that mended families can mend our churches; and mended churches can mend our communities; and mended communities can mend our nation.

One of the programs sponsored by **IN MY HEART, MINISTRIES** is the Coffee-Klatch study group where ordinary women meet to spend time before God and in His word. We are women who help each other maintain focus in an ever-changing society. Additionally, a quarterly newsletter of the same name is preparing for circulation, offering timely articles and insights for women who are actively seeking to know God.

There will be a **POWER IN THE PAIN** seminar coming to a town near you. Our readers are encouraged to attend. You can request a meeting at your church or women's organization.

We, at **IN MY HEART, MINISTRIES,** request your prayerful support of our efforts. If you need more information, would like to order the *Coffee-Klatch*, or would like to request a meeting, please feel free to contact us today at:

IN MY HEART, MINISTRIES
P.O. BOX 946
LANHAM MD 20703-0946
(301) 794-7366

IN MY HEART, MINISTRIES
"Do all that is in thine heart..." 1 Samuel 14:7

PRAYER REQUESTS

I have committed myself to partner with you, my reader, in prayer. If you have any special concerns you would like me to pray for specifically, please write them below, and mail this page to me.

Also, please use this space to share your comments of testimonies; I look forward to hearing about the impact of this book.